THE DEAD DETECTIVE

IN

THE CORPSE THAT SANG

THE DEAD DETECTIVE

IN

THE CORPSE THAT SANG

by Felix Bogarte™

Published 2003 by Books Noir Ltd, Glasgow

Text written by Joan Love and Mhairi MacDiarmid,
based on a story by Mhairi MacDiarmid

A CIP catalogue for this book is available from the British Library

ISBN 1-904684-03-3

Printed and bound in the EU

www.booksnoir.com
www.deaddetective.com
info@deaddetective.com

CONTENTS

WHO'S WHO IN DEAD DETECTIVE LAND

WHO IS CHARLIE CHRISTIAN?

12 year-old Charlie Christian is a born detective – and has been given the opportunity to prove himself. The Court Of Ghouls, who exist in a twilight zone between life and death have decreed that the Dead Detective, Hank Kane be sentenced to fight crime in Charlie's very own city of Glasgow! And, as Hank Kane cannot be trusted to solve cases honestly he has been instructed to take on someone he can train as a detective – someone like Charlie Christian.

WHO IS ANNIE?

Ten year-old Annie, or "Ace" as her brother, Charlie, insists on calling her is the world's most reluctant detective. To say that she doesn't share her brother's love of all things detective would be putting it mildly – the whole investigative "scene" bores her senseless.

WHO IS THE GRIM REAPER?

The Grim Reaper, or TG as he likes to be known,

really enjoys his work. He loves the perks of his job, annoying Hank, partying and fiddling his expenses.

SO, WHO IS THE DEAD DETECTIVE?

The Dead Detective is Hank Kane, a crooked cop, killed in the line of duty in Los Angeles in the 1950s. Instead of passing straight over to the other side, however, Hank finds himself facing the Court Of Ghouls, who have decided that he'll have to pay for his habit of planting evidence on suspects. They sentence him to fighting crime, using only honest methods, until they are convinced that he's learnt his lesson. They instruct The Grim Reaper to keep an eye on Hank. It isn't that they don't totally trust Hank – it's just that they don't trust him at all!

Hank's other problem is his appearance. He's a skeleton! During daylight hours he has no flesh on his bones (well, he *is* dead!) and so has to stay out of sight. At night, however, providing he drinks some of his chemical compound, flesh returns to his bones and he looks almost normal. "Almost" because Hank died fifty years previously and has been catapulted forward in time to 2003.

CHAPTER 1

SLEEPING IN THE SUNLIGHT

IT was two o'clock in the morning and the street was dark and silent, except for the occasional howl of a stray cat. There was no wind that night and no unusual or distinctive noises. Yet something had awakened the Dead Detective, Hank Kane.

He lay motionless for a while, staring up at the ceiling, listening for a clue as to what had caused him to wake up. He must have had the radio on earlier, as he could still hear some dumb tune ringing in his head. He glanced at his alarm clock and sighed heavily. He'd only been asleep for a few hours but he knew he'd find it almost impossible to doze off again.

He picked up the remote control from where he had placed it earlier by the side of the bed and hit one of the channels. May as well watch some TV, he thought, maybe some dumb schmuck will send me straight back to sleep!

His young assistants, Charlie and Annie, had persuaded Hank to get the TV. As they spent a considerable amount of time in Hank's office, they felt that the least he could do was have a decent TV!

The screen came to life and the room was filled with colour. A discussion programme was on; the kind where people sit together on orange, leather chairs and have in-depth conversations about the use of the colour red on a book cover. He wondered if these people got a fee for doing such shows. He hoped not. He decided the programme would annoy him so much that he'd be kept *awake*, rather than lulled back to sleep.

He flicked over to the next channel. A black and white movie! Brilliant! One from the 1950s, too. The movie was set in New York and was about reporters competing for the story of a killer who was terrorising the city. Hank felt instantly at home.

To Charlie and Annie, these films were set in the 'olden days' but to Hank it always felt more like 'now' than the present day did. The camera pulled in for a close up and he recognised Dana Andrews and Vincent Price. He watched for a few more minutes before becoming restless. He'd seen the movie too many times for it to hold his attention. He knew the script off by heart.

Hank must have pressed the remote control without knowing it. All of a sudden, a late night music show came on, with a group of jazz musicians who looked like they were having the time of their life. He liked 1950s jazz and decided to watch it for a while.

The band finished their number and slowed the tempo right down for their next offering. A young, blond woman walked slowly into the middle of the studio, and took the mike. She started to sing, her husky voice perfectly matching the instruments accompanying her.

Hank leant forward, squinting at the screen. There was something very familiar about this dame. He felt like he knew her. The way her hair curled to her shoulders, the green of her eyes, the curve of her lips. He turned on his bedside lamp and swung his legs out of bed, pulling on his dressing gown as he did so. He was still unaccustomed to the chill of the night air in Glasgow, and his skeletal frame was useless at keeping the cold out!

The singer was coming to the end of her set

now, her hips swaying in perfect time to the music. Her long fingernails curled around the microphone stand as she finished the last note of a faintly familiar song. She then bowed her head in response to the smattering of applause in the studio.

When she lifted her head and smiled her thanks towards the camera, Hank knew why she looked familiar. It was Rachel. No-one else smiled like that. No-one sang like that! And that song! What was it called again? That's right, *Sleeping In The Sunlight*.

That sweet soothing voice was the one he heard in his head every day, the same one he tried so hard to forget. Man, it was like it haunted him. One side of Rachel's mouth lifted slightly higher than the other, and a dimple formed on the left side of her cheek. Rachel Corless!

Hank couldn't believe what he was seeing. He thought of recording the programme on the VCR his young assistant, Charlie, had talked him into buying, but the programme was nearly over. And besides, he had no idea how to use the VCR!

Moments later the show finished and Hank began scanning the list of credits. However, he soon realised that the names of the guest stars must have appeared at the beginning of the programme. The credits Hank was now reading were only the producers, directors and make-up artists, like he was interested!

Deep down, however, he didn't need to read her name in the credits. He knew it was Rachel. What really freaked him out was that her face on the screen had been decomposing, ever so slightly! The flesh was… well… melting, or so it seemed. In fact, her face looked just like his own when his flesh-preserving 'potion' was wearing off. Come to think of it, nobody on that show had looked particularly healthy.

He sank back down onto his bed; all thoughts of sleep were long gone. He shook his head in disbelief. Rachel. *His* beautiful Rachel. It couldn't be her.

Hank remembered how she used to sing with the band in the dance hall the cops went to after work. She and Hank had even written that song, *Sleeping In The Sunlight*, together. It was a tribute to cops they'd known; the ones who hadn't made it to the end of their shifts without some low-life shooting them dead in the streets of LA.

Rachel had been a detective with the LAPD. She'd worked alongside Hank and had done her job brilliantly. But one gloriously sunny summer's day she'd been gunned down by a worthless bank robber. She had tried to help one of the terrified bank tellers but had ended up in the robber's direct line of fire.

Hank had been one of the first on the scene and remembered how he'd found the stark contrast between the warm sunshine outside the bank and the coldness of Rachel's hand very hard to deal with.

Rachel had been shot at point blank range. Hank found out later that the robber had actually held the barrel of the gun against her temple and squeezed the trigger. God, she must have been so scared for that second before she sank to the floor, her death instantaneous.

Hank could hardly bear to think of the scene even now. How he'd held the young woman in his arms, watched by other hard-bitten detectives, many with tears in their eyes.

Everyone had liked Rachel. She'd been a good

person and a great detective. She and Hank had shared an understanding. They'd been partners, both in and out of work, and though the words had never been spoken it was understood that they'd marry some day. And then she was killed. Blown away by a low-life who wasn't fit to tie her shoelaces.

Hank had found her killer after working tirelessly night and day. He hadn't slept until he'd arrested the guy and seen him stand trial.

The agony of it was, despite the robber having been identified by dozens of witnesses, he'd been acquitted! Some smart lawyer had got him off on a 'technicality'. In fact, the case had been thrown out of court by the judge, without even allowing the jury to deliver their verdict! Some said the judge had been bribed. But who could prove it? After that Hank Kane's world had fallen apart.

Up until then, Hank Kane had been one of the most honest cops LA had ever known. He refused bribes from gangsters. He believed in the fair treatment of prisoners. He hated other cops who planted evidence and beat confessions out of suspects or who cheated in any way.

Heck, he even believed in 'innocent until proven guilty'.

In Hank's eyes, cops who cheated betrayed the whole idea of law and order. They betrayed the public and betrayed themselves. He was one of the few cops who had no trouble giving evidence against corrupt cops in court. And yet he was not only tolerated by his fellow officers but was actually respected by them because he was one of the bravest guys on the force. And, despite sticking to his own rules on fairness, he put away more bad guys than anyone else.

In Rachel, Hank had spotted a rookie detective who was one of the few determined to do things the 'Hank Kane way'. It was natural that they'd grown close. They were soul mates. But when she died, the good guy in Hank died, too.

He'd thrown himself into his work. Any niceties he may have possessed in the past were now non-existent. He spent every waking hour trying to clean up the streets of LA and he didn't care how he did it. He was in mourning and criminals, gangsters and low-lifes in general were made to mourn with him. For the first time in a generation, the streets were safe and the bad guys were the ones who were scared.

The rest of the police department took their lead from Hank. He was promoted to captain. The mayor praised him. The public loved him. What a fool he'd been all these years, he'd often thought, to have ever tried to play so fair with Evil. Evil needed its butt kicked and he was in just the mood to do it - forever. He didn't care if he lived or died and that made him brave and dangerous. Hank's one-man war was ferocious. It couldn't have gone on forever. And it didn't.

Hank had been shot dead while chasing a robber in the street. He'd found himself in front of the Court Of Ghouls, who'd condemned him for cheating and becoming everything he hated. They'd sentenced him to solving crime honestly and sent him to Glasgow to do just that. Why Glasgow? One of the judges at the Court had spun a globe; he'd closed his eyes and his finger had landed on Glasgow – it could have been anywhere.

But now Rachel had appeared! Hank had just watched her perform on TV! Though Hank knew the situation was impossible, he allowed himself a trip down memory lane, and eventually drifted into a fitful sleep.

He woke late the next morning, roused by the sound of commuters scurrying along Gordon Street from Central Station on their way to work. He convinced himself that he'd dreamed the Rachel incident. He dragged himself out of bed and looked at his reflection in the bathroom mirror. "Mirror, Mirror…" he asked sarcastically, still not used to his skeletal appearance. "Jeez, I look like death," he said.

This thought always raised a twisted smile on Hank's face. The reflection which stared back at him from the mirror had no flesh, it was merely a skull. His eye sockets were empty, except for a red glow, and his teeth were far too large for his face.

Hank's 'dream' of Rachel ensured she was very much in his thoughts that day. What would she make of him now? He wondered. Here he was, fifty years on, running a private detective agency, set up for him by the Court Of Ghouls. He even had a minder, none other than the Grim Reaper himself.

Hank was the only employee at the agency but he was 'helped' by his assistants, twelve-year old Charlie and his ten-year old sister, Annie. This was another rule set by the court. Hank wasn't allowed to offer them any help. Instead, he had to leave Charlie and Annie to solve the cases for themselves.

Hank's role, the Court had insisted, was to train them in the art of honest detective work. If he succeeded in this task, the Court would be convinced that he really had gone back to solving crime the 'Hank Kane Way'.

Hank examined his reflection again, sighed and shook his head. Still, he supposed he should look on the bright side. He hadn't needed a shave in months.

He went back into his bedroom to get dressed and immediately spotted the dark, cloaked figure sitting on the edge of his bed. The hood of the cloak was pulled forward, completely covering his face, and his body was swathed entirely in black. The stench of death was all around him and a scythe lay on the floor by his side.

"Hey, Grim," said Hank as he entered the room.

CHAPTER 2

PROTECTING ANGEL

THE Grim Reaper (or TG as he was called) had been assigned by the Court of Ghouls to accompany Hank on his earthly forays into the criminal world. However, Hank had recently caught the Grim Reaper doing something he shouldn't have. This meant therefore that Hank had something on him.

The murder of a Glasgow gangster had taken place and the Grim Reaper had gone to the scene to collect the gangster's soul. Unfortunately, the event had clashed with a rock concert TG had desperately wanted to attend.

The gangster was taking far too long to die for TG's liking so he'd given him a helping hand and speeded up the gangster's end. Hank had become aware of this, partly due to his own instincts and partly due to TG's blabbing down at *The Cesspit* nightclub - the trendy club for Glasgow's ghost and ghouls. The price of Hank's silence was that TG had to be a little more helpful than was allowed by the Court when Hank was on a case.

Hank also discovered that TG was a frustrated follower of fashion who hated the black cloak his occupation forced him to wear. The Grim Reaper reckoned he could have been a big hit with the ladies but his unfortunate garb and blackened teeth meant that his romantic opportunities were thin on the ground! And the stench of death just could not be disguised, no matter how much *Armani* he doused himself in!

Hank left TG to sleep off a hangover and made his way into his office. Charlie would be dropping by tonight and Hank wondered if he'd managed to find out anything more about the murder they were currently investigating. He'd come to grudgingly admire his young assistant, Charlie (though he did his best to hide that fact from 'The Kid' as he called him).

They'd been working on the case for over a week now and hadn't made much headway. A body had been found in a nearby graveyard. Nothing strange there – except this one hadn't been buried! Albie Merrins had been fatally stabbed and his body placed in the graveyard. It was pretty strange that the body had been placed beneath a huge statue of an angel whose wings seemed to stretch protectively over his body, albeit too late.

The Merrins family in general, and Albie in particular, was well known to both local police and local criminals. The one thing both sides of the law and order war agreed on was a world without Albie was a better world.

He had a police record as long as your arm that had started off with petty crime when he was a teenager. He had progressed to the odd breaking and entering job. Eventually he'd been caught holding up an off licence with a sawn-off shotgun and served his first jail sentence.

Money lending followed and he soon became both hated and feared in the community. Albie was no Robin Hood. The money wasn't always stolen from the rich – and never given to the poor. The question wasn't, '*Who* would kill him?' but 'Who *wouldn't* kill him?' thought Hank.

Something no-one except Hank seemed to know, though, was that Merrins had a niece, Sally Parkinson. She'd left the area many years previously, ashamed of the Merrins connection. A pretty girl, she'd moved to London, where she'd met and married John Parkinson, a rich businessman.

Recently, she'd told Hank, she'd decided she wanted to make peace with her family. She'd tried to get in touch with Albie, but it was too late. When she'd found out her uncle had been killed, she'd flown immediately to Glasgow from London.

Having been brought up not to trust the police, she'd said she'd found herself directed to Private Detective Hank Kane's office. She wouldn't say who by.

Sally said that she was desperate for the killer to be caught before he killed again. She stressed that point over and over. Meanwhile, she'd found accommodation in one of the better parts of the city, staying well away from the area she'd grown up in. While she'd obviously become very nostalgic about her family, poverty wasn't something she was sentimental about, thought Hank.

Hank had been impressed with the gangster's niece. She was classy and decent; everything Albie had never been. That was the only reason he'd agreed to take on the case. That, and the certain knowledge that the Court Of Ghouls would give him no choice!

Of course, it hadn't escaped Hank's notice that Sally Parkinson was very pretty, so pretty it was impossible not to stare at her. In fact there was something angelic about her. Hers was a very pure beauty, the only tiny imperfection being a birthmark the shape of a heart on her left cheek. She tried to cover this up with expensive make up but Hank noticed it all the same.

Hank felt obliged to produce results. But so far he and Charlie had uncovered nothing. And time was pressing on.

CHAPTER 3

BORN TO IT

CHARLIE read the note his mum had left for him on the kitchen table. It said that she was in bed, having just finished another night shift at the local hospital where she worked as a nurse. He didn't have a problem with the bit about picking up some shopping from the supermarket. However, he *did* have a problem with the bit about taking his sister, Annie, to the skating rink where her friend was having a birthday party.

Annie and her friends drove him mad, always coming into his bedroom to ask all sorts of dumb questions and giggling and whispering as only girls do. On her own, 'Ace' (as Charlie called her) wasn't too bad; she'd even helped Charlie out on his last case. But Charlie liked to think of himself as a super detective in the making and he didn't like to have to admit that he sometimes needed help, from his sister of all people.

Her help had actually been crucial in solving a couple of the Dead Detective's last cases. Still, he'd better make sure he delivered her to the ice rink safely. Mum's anger wasn't something to look forward to!

Annie shifted in her seat. The bus journey was taking forever and she was really bored. She was also curious. She looked at Charlie carefully. He was up to something. Again. She just knew it. He couldn't wait to drop her off at the ice rink and go off and do something interesting. She knew he had no intention of telling her just what he was up to but she had every intention of finding out.

Annie knew the telltale signs that her brother was 'on a case' with Hank. He was cheerful, distracted – and eager to dump her. Annie had enjoyed helping Charlie and Hank in the past but she knew that Charlie felt she was better than him at detective work. So, she waved goodbye to him at the bus stop and went inside to meet her friends. One of the other girl's mothers had promised to drop her back home so Charlie wasn't needed for the return journey.

This was just as well, for Charlie was indeed 'up to something' as Annie put it. She was right. He was working on a new case with Hank.

Charlie was a keen detective, and he was quite happy to spend his school holidays digging around for clues, desperate as he was to prove himself to Hank.

Charlie made his way back to the graveyard where Albie Merrins' body had been found a week previously. This would be his fourth visit to the spot and so far he had come up with nothing. However, he knew, just knew, that something crucial was missing.

He stood on the exact spot where Merrins' body had been placed and read the words inscribed on the gravestones immediately next to him. They were the words of families saying goodbye to their loved ones; dates and occasional quotes from the Bible. Nothing more.

He took his notebook and pen from his pocket and started to write down surnames. Surnames from the fifteen or so grave stones which could be seen from where Merrins had been found. You never know, he thought, perhaps someone had placed Merrins' body here at this very spot deliberately. Maybe a relative of one of Merrins' victims had put his body near the grave of a loved one, as if in revenge. And like Hank always said, at the beginning of a case, you have to take any train of thought for even just a couple of stops. It's the only way to come across clues.

He wrote down dates too, in case any of those should prove significant. He knew from Hank's contact at the local police department that forensics hadn't been able to come up with very much. The grass and dirt found in Merrins' hair and under his fingernails had matched the grass and dirt from the graveyard but that didn't exactly tell them anything they didn't know. It didn't tell them for sure where he'd been killed. Plus, the murder weapon still hadn't been found.

A youngish man with curly, brown hair approached Charlie. He wore denims, trainers and a black leather jacket. He was also wearing a dog collar.

"Can I help you, young man?" asked the minister. He had seen Charlie at the same spot a couple of times before and wondered what brought him there. Charlie turned and smiled, putting his notebook back into his pocket.

"No thanks," he said. "I was just leaving. I'm

doing a project at school on, eh...." He floundered for a moment, trying to think quickly. "...on, em, old buildings in Glasgow." He recovered himself and turned to look in the direction of the church. "It's a couple of hundred years old, isn't it?" he stammered.

In truth, Charlie had no idea of the age of the church but, judging by the state of disrepair some of the gravestones were in, he doubted if he was very far out.

"Yes, I believe it's about a hundred and eighty years old, so compared to that I'm fairly young!" the minister smiled. "I've only moved here fairly recently so I can't say I know too much about the history of the church, or its people, as yet. But I do intend to learn. I find it fascinating just wondering around the graveyard and searching the church grounds."

"'Searching'? What do you hope to find?" asked Charlie, intrigued.

"Myself, I hope to find myself," replied the minister.

"Yourself?" asked Charlie, bewildered.

"Oh, you know what I mean - 'peace of mind'. We all want to find our true selves, our real selves. We all want to find the person we really were meant to be, as designed by God, not the person we end up becoming, moulded by circumstances."

"Right," said Charlie nodding wisely. That's what he usually did when adults said things he didn't understand.

The minister began to walk down the path towards the gate and Charlie joined him.

"Perhaps we could help each other," suggested the minister. "You can tell me what you've learnt in pursuit of your project and I can share any information I pick up with you."

Charlie nodded. No point in making an enemy of the minister. Who knows how much more time he'd need to spend here? And, it would be nice to have an ally.

"Sure, sounds fair to me," said Charlie as he opened the gate. "I have to go and write up my notes just now, but I'll probably be back."

The minister pulled the gate shut and made a face as it squeaked. "Must remember to buy some oil," he said to himself. He leant on the gate and offered his outstretched hand to Charlie.

"Jason Harvey," he introduced himself. "*Reverend* Jason Harvey, I should say," he smiled.

Charlie shook the minister's hand.

"Charlie Christian," he said. "Nice to meet you."

"Nice to meet you, Charlie. And what a great surname you have! I wish I was blessed with a name like that! Goodness, some people strive all their lives to become 'Christians' – and others are just born to it. I'm jealous, Charlie, I really am!" He laughed.

"Oh I don't know," said Charlie, "I think I'd prefer your name!"

"Oh yes," said the minister, quietly, "*My* name. I'll look forward to speaking with you again next week. Did you know we have a youth club for ten to fourteen year olds every Friday night? You should come along, you'd enjoy it."

Charlie nodded and started to walk down the road.

"Yeah, I might just do that, Reverend."

CHAPTER 4

DETAILS

CHARLIE returned home and went straight to his bedroom. He opened his wardrobe door as wide as he could so that he was able to see the board that hung inside the door. He had re-created the crime scene, as seen on all the best police programmes, starting with a picture of the victim cut from the local newspaper.

He had also pinned up details of the crime, again as reported in the paper, and a word-for-word account of what Forensics had told Hank. Merrin's death had been a major event in Glasgow and one of the newspapers had published a whole page of letters and articles from people who wanted to write and say something about the man. Charlie had kept the page and had input all the writers' surnames into his PC.

"Details," he could almost hear Hank's voice saying, "Details that count and details that don't count. Which is which? You don't know at the time. But if you don't note *every* detail, you'll *never* know."

Charlie sat down at his computer and began to input the names he had copied from the gravestones. He also entered the dates he had scribbled down and then saved all the information. Next, he asked the computer to find a match with the names from the letters in the newspaper. One name was thrown up. Sinclair. He looked at his hand-written notes to see what information he had taken from the gravestone.

Geoffrey Sinclair
Born: 25.2.1937
Died: 31.8.1997
Gone but not forgotten

"Short and sweet," thought Charlie as he opened a drawer. Surely there must have been more information inscribed on the gravestone than he'd written down. He'd call back there on his way to Hank's that evening just in case. He didn't want to miss anything.

He pulled out the letters' page he had kept from the newspaper and scanned it for one signed 'Sinclair'. He found it halfway down the right hand side of the page. It was the shortest letter on the page; if it could even be described as a letter.

Farewell, then, to Mr Merrins.
Romans: chapter 12: verse 19
M Sinclair

"It's a quote from the Bible," thought Charlie. He didn't have a Bible that he could look up to see what it meant. He'd had one as a small boy but had lost it some years ago and had not in all honesty spent a lot of time trying to find it.

Annie would have one! She kept everything; old toys, her Barbie dolls and even her own baby shoes and socks in tissue paper. She was a dead cert to have kept the Bible mum had given her.

He went quickly to her room and began looking through her things, taking care not to mess anything up. Third drawer down and he got lucky; carefully folded white lace gloves, what looked like, but couldn't possibly be, christening cake, and placed neatly beside it, her little white Bible. It was almost identical to the one he'd received from his mum. He stifled a pang of guilt, slammed the drawer door shut and took Ace's Bible back to his own room. He turned quickly to Romans: 12 and 19 and read the verse aloud:

> "For it is written, vengeance is mine;
> I will repay saith the Lord."

"Vengeance," thought Charlie. The use of the word 'vengeance' was interesting though the way the verse was worded implied that God would be the guy doing the repaying. Now just why would someone quote that particular verse as though it were some sort of message to Merrins?

Obviously someone had a grudge against Merrins. Not every grudge against Albie Merrins would be a motive for killing him, thought Charlie. If that were true, then half the city would be suspects. Still it did seem weird to Charlie that someone who knew his Bible quotes seemed to have forgotten the bits about love and forgiveness. Now there was someone in need of a minister or a priest.

Charlie puzzled over the verse for a few more

minutes then put the Bible into his rucksack, along with his notebook and a few other items he wanted to show Hank when he went to visit him later that evening.

CHAPTER 5

STILL A BESTSELLER

HANK took his hat from the stand in his office and shot a glance at TG. "I'm off to *The Cesspit* for a sarsaparilla, wanna come?"

TG was lounging on the sofa but got up immediately. He loved socialising. "Sure, I'd love to, but isn't Charlie coming over tonight?"

"We'll be back in plenty of time," replied Hank, locking the office door. "Just need to get some air to help me think."

Hank checked his appearance quickly in the glass section of the door. His special chemical drink had done its stuff! Flesh had returned to his face and he looked almost normal. Not that he needed to look great for *The Cesspit*! He was still a bit pale and he'd probably dropped a collar size or two but it was still miles better than the skeletal look.

There were a number of cash points in Buchanan Street, just around the corner from Hank's office. Most of the points were on their own, however there were a few located side by side. *The Cesspit* was near these and could be found with the right ghoul to guide you.

A short journey down a passageway, a sharp left and two sharp rights took you to the door of the nightclub. A welcome sign hung above the doorway to *The Cesspit*, the pitch black entrance hall disturbed only by the occasional puff of smoke. The smoke wasn't dry ice, as might be seen in other nightclubs, but clouds created by the pungent aroma of death and rotting flesh which came from the customers.

The place was like a second home to the Grim Reaper. Hank used to think that TG was just another customer but he had learnt that TG actually owned the place. Nobody knew how to make a buck like TG.

"Darn," thought Hank as they turned into Buchanan Street. A guy was using one of the cash points and was swaying all over the place, obviously very drunk. This particular cash point was a shortcut into *The Cesspit*. TG was one of the few who knew the secret code to tap into the panel that would open the entrance.

They'd have to pretend to be withdrawing money from one of the other cash points until the man had gone. Hank sighed. It *would* have to be one of those people who had no idea what they were doing. I mean, what could be so difficult? Key in your PIN number, tell the machine how much cash you want, put the dough in your wallet and leave. Whatever this guy was doing, though, was far from straightforward. When Hank finally saw him pocket the cash, he breathed a sigh of relief.

"Darn! What now?" TG looked on in disbelief as the man brought out yet another bankcard and prepared to carry out yet another transaction! TG tapped the guy on the shoulder with his scythe. The man turned around and almost fell over when he saw who had tapped him.

"You gonna be much longer, fella?" asked TG in the most menacing voice he could muster.

Hank hid a smile. TG could be quite useful at times.

"No, no," said the guy, as he tried to back away, tripping over his own feet and falling backwards towards the cash point as he did so.

"No, I was just leaving. It's all yours," he stammered, desperate to get away.

"Hey buddy," shouted TG as the frightened man began to walk away, "you forgot your card."

Later, when the terrified man told the story to his friends, he said he didn't know which was worse; the hollow sockets which stood out against the stark whiteness of the freak's face or the feel of its hand as it pressed the bankcard into his. Its hands were as cold as the earth with scaly, slimy, nails like talons; indescribable really. His friends looked at him in disbelief and shrugged. They had warned him before about his drinking habits.

Hank, meanwhile, had wasted no time and was now walking into the nightclub. TG shuffled along behind. Suddenly, Hank tripped over a huge pair of feet which stuck out from beneath a table. The feet belonged to Frankie, a good friend of TG's. Hank regained his balance and straightened his tie.

"Sorry, Frankie," he shouted above the noise of the music. Frankie smiled, raised his sarsaparilla in Hank's direction and adjusted one of his neck bolts. Frankie Steen was a minor celebrity. After all, he'd had a book written about him more than a hundred years ago and it was *still* a bestseller!

Everyone had thought that Mary Shelly's

book, *Frankenstein* had been based on her imagination. Heck, even *she'd* thought she'd made it all up! Little did she know that Frankie (as he preferred to be known) was very real. He'd thought of suing Mary Shelly because he never agreed that he was a monster. Sure, he could lose his head once in a while but only when the stitching around his neck unravelled!

Hank and TG headed straight for the bar. Oliver, the barman, was serving six people at the same time, a feat he found pretty easy since he was the proud owner of six arms. His sister, Lily, being similarly endowed, was the reigning darts' champion *and* pool champion, playing both games at the same time!

"What'll it be, Hank, TG?" asked Oliver, "double sarsaparillas?"

"Very funny," replied Hank as he and TG sat down at a table. He hated the fact that dead people couldn't drink hard liquor. What remained of their earthly bodies was simply unable to absorb the alcohol, so *The Cesspit* did a roaring trade in sarsaparillas. Hank had to grudgingly admit he was developing a taste for the stuff.

He looked around. Shame, really, some of these guys couldn't find work any more. The film industry had developed so much in recent years that guys like the *Weirdowolf* and *Count Dracula* found themselves unemployed. They just weren't scary any more. Many of them often pestered TG with screenplay ideas, hoping the movie company he was setting up might be able to use them.

Hank sipped on his drink and looked around. His eyes rested on the TV screen above the bar. Another one of those 'reality TV' shows. Try as he might, Hank simply failed to see the attraction of watching ordinary people sitting around in an ordinary house and make ordinary conversation with each other. Now, if the TV companies were to make a programme on life in *The Cesspit*, the viewers would maybe see something just a little more interesting.

He looked over at the Grim Reaper and stirred his drink with his straw. "So, TG," he began, "you gonna tell me who dunnit?"

TG looked back at him.

"Done what, Hank?"

"Come on, TG, don't treat me like I'm some

dumb kid. You know what I'm talking about. Who killed Albie Merrins?"

"Aw, Hank, you know I'm not supposed to tell you. You know the Court wouldn't be happy if…"

"Fine, fine," said Hank, putting up his hand in dismissal. "Next time I'm speaking to those guys I'll have a word in their ears about someone who… how shall I put it? … crossed over to the other side a little quicker than they should have." He leant back in his chair.

TG said nothing.

Hank's eyes flickered once again to the TV screen. He almost dropped his glass. The game show was over and in its place was Rachel! His Rachel! Singing her little heart out and looking unbelievably stunning in a floor length, red dress!

He screwed up his eyes and tried to focus more clearly. Was it really Rachel? Were his eyes deceiving him? Was it simply that he wanted it to be Rachel so much he was convincing himself that it *was* her? She had finished her song now and the show's host was walking onto the stage to thank her. He strained to catch her name.

TG chose that same moment to whisper the name of the killer in Hank's ear. Hank jumped back, furious at TG's interruption.

"You clown!" he shouted. "I was trying to hear what the guy on the TV was saying. Are you completely stupid? How am I ever going to find out who that girl was? Why did you have to speak just at that precise moment?"

He slammed his drink down on the table and stood up.

TG, confused by the onslaught, tried to protest.

"You *did* ask me a question, Hank, remember..."

"Yeah, but I did *not* need you to speak just then, did I?" He shook his head. "Never mind, I've had enough for one night anyway. I'm leaving. Oh, and one more thing, TG, get yourself some breath freshener."

"What's your problem, Hank? You wanna know something about some dame from the TV? Just ask me, pal."

"How would you know where to find out about her?"

"Well, let's just say that the TV channel you were watching was not a...regular TV channel."

"What do you mean?" asked Hank, realising that once again TG was ahead of the game.

"Well, the channel you've been watching is called, 'Dead Guy TV'."

"Dead Guy TV?" parroted Hank, exasperated.

"Yeah, it's a new venture. Very experimental. Not even sure if we've got all the technical hitches solved yet. Tried to beam it to the TV in your office the other night, Hank. But you never mentioned it. So I guess in here is the only place it can be viewed, for the moment."

Hank sat back down. So he hadn't dreamed it after all. He sipped his drink once more. He thought about what TG had said.

"So let me get this straight, TG. You've started a TV channel for all us dead folks, right?"

"Right! I'm always thinking!" exclaimed TG, full of admiration for himself.

"Well, I guess there was a gap in *that* market!"

"You better believe it! But, until I can beam it out to other TVs, then the ratings won't be winning prizes!"

"So, only dead folks will be able to get this channel, when it becomes available I mean?"

"Right again, Hank. Look around you. These

guys need more than sarsaparilla. Look at all the talent here. I hear them sing, make jokes, draw paintings. Think about it! What other TV channel could bring you new poetry from TS Elliot, new plays by Shakespeare, new comedies by Charlie Chaplin! My contacts among the dead are second to none! Hey, in business, you gotta do what you know."

Hank was fascinated. What a great idea! He had to hand it to TG. He was certainly onto something.

"So you know everyone on that show?" he asked.

"Sure I do. I let the guys who run it do all the bookings and stuff. I'm an ideas man, Hank. I leave the details to others. But if you wanna know about someone on the show, I could tell you. But trust me. It's better you take care of that yourself this time."

"But you owe me one, TG."

"Yeah, I know I do. But trust me on this one, Hank. The Court Of Ghouls is paying more attention than usual. They'd know I helped you. And you'd be back at square one. But, there's no law against *Charlie* helping you though. Let's use that loophole until they seal it up!"

"Yeah, right," snapped Hank, "like, the kid would know where to start."

"What's the matter, Hank? You not teaching him well? He's been on four cases with you so far and I'd say he's done all right. Trust him a bit. And besides, maybe he won't always know when he's helping you."

Hank looked at TG with something near despair.

"You just pull all the strings, don't you, TG," said Hank, even more aware than ever that his fate was in TG's bony hands.

"What a great idea, Hank! A puppet show for my TV channel! Thanks! I owe you, buddy!

"Forgive me if I don't wait up for payback time."

CHAPTER 6

THE WATCHMAN

CHARLIE was outside the office when Hank returned. He grunted what passed for a greeting in 'the kid's' direction and made his way upstairs to the office.

Hi yourself, thought Charlie as he walked behind. Hank looked like someone who was having a good day – Not!

Charlie sat across the desk from Hank and emptied out the contents of his rucksack. Hank pushed his hair out of his eyes and made himself focus on his assistant. After all, it wasn't Charlie's fault Hank had an idiot for a friend.

"So, Charlie, what have you got for me?"

Charlie showed him the evidence he had collected so far. Evidence against *whom*, he still didn't know, but he knew he'd get there in the end.

"...so there's definitely a connection between the letter writer and the inscription on the gravestone," said Charlie. "I just need to find out who 'M Sinclair' is and why he or she quoted Romans: 12 and 19 in their letter."

"Sounds like a job for the padre, Reverend Harvey," suggested Hank. "If anyone would know their Bible, *he* would. I remember hearing some of these preacher guys on my car radio back in the 1950s. Jeez, they'd sure scare the bejeebas outta ya! All that talk of hellfire and –"

"Vengeance?" finished Charlie.

"Yeah!"

"I've heard of some of those American preachers. But they can't all be like that, Hank."

"No I'm sure they aren't. But if you want help with the Bible, then a preacher's what you need. Now let's look at that quote, Charlie."

Charlie reached for the Bible. Only it wasn't there!

"Shoot," said Charlie. "I am in *so* much trouble."

"What's wrong, kid?" asked Hank.

"I've lost my sister's Bible. I called in at the graveyard again on my way over here tonight to double check if I had missed anything on the Sinclair gravestone and I must have dropped it then." He began packing everything else away. "I'll have to go and look for it, Hank. If Ace finds out it's missing, I'm dead. I'll call by tomorrow night, if that's okay."

"Sure," Hank nodded, "and Charlie?"

"Yes?" replied Charlie, turning around.

"Miss anything on the gravestone?"

"Oh, yeah, sorry. Another scripture is quoted. Matthew something or other; haven't had time to look it up yet. And if I don't find Ace's Bible I won't be alive long enough to do that!"

And with that he was gone.

Charlie turned right, down the road leading to the church and graveyard. It was really dark, not helped by the fact that the street lamps were broken. They'd been out of action for weeks now and nobody seemed to care enough to do anything about having them fixed. He had a torch with him so he should be able to find a white Bible without too many problems. Or so he tried to convince himself.

He climbed over a broken part of the wall which was much lower than the rest and stood on the grass looking across the cemetery. He shivered. Though he wouldn't have admitted it to anyone else, Charlie was just a tiny bit scared.

A graveyard, no lights and a spooky old church overlooking the whole scene was just a wee bit too much for him. He thought of leaving and coming back in the morning when it was daylight but the thought of Ace discovering the loss tonight (which would just be his luck) made him dig into his rucksack for his torch. He made his way to the area of the cemetery where he'd been earlier that evening.

Charlie switched on his torch and, feeling like a criminal himself, made his way along the path. He stopped beside the grave of 'G Sinclair' and shone the torch around. He couldn't see the Bible. Suddenly he found himself in total darkness. The torch had gone out.

Shoot, he thought to himself. I thought I'd replaced the batteries fairly recently. He shook the torch to see if it would work but the light stayed out. He decided he should go. There was no point in staying here, now he couldn't see a thing, only the shapes of the headstones, statues and branches of trees. A wind was building up, and the branches were starting to make shapes. Eerie shapes. "Stop it, Charlie," he said to himself. "You're letting your imagination run away with you."

He heard a noise. It was a crunching noise as though someone was walking across the gravel.

Charlie froze. What would anyone be doing here at this time of night? Maybe it was the young minister he'd met earlier today. He turned in the direction of the noise and squinted in the darkness.

Charlie thought his heart would stop. It definitely wasn't the minister, not unless he'd grown his hair long since this afternoon and gained an extra foot or so in height. The guy that was now heading in Charlie's direction had long flowing, white hair and was slightly hunched over. Charlie could just about make out that he was a huge, imposing, older man. Though he walked slowly, his strides were so long he was standing in front of Charlie before he could even think of trying to hide.

Forcing himself out of his trance, Charlie turned to run. He had to get out of here. Whoever this guy was, he certainly didn't look overly friendly.

Charlie ran blindly, hoping against hope that

he was heading in the direction of the exit from the graveyard. Behind him, he knew the man was coming after him, not running, but striding purposefully in his wake, as though he knew exactly where he was going, despite the darkness.

Charlie ran as though his heart would burst, finally able to make out the shape of the gate. But, just as he approached the exit, he tripped over one of his laces and was flung forward. He fell really hard, hitting his head off a sharp latch on the gate. He felt the stinging pain and crumpled on the grass, unable to get up.

The man approached. Charlie looked up and could feel the blood running from his head down into his eyes. The man loomed over him. Huge. He must be at least seven foot tall, thought Charlie, and look how big his hands are.

The man bent over Charlie, hands outstretched ready to place them around Charlie's neck. They won't have any trouble pinning my murder on you, was Charlie's last waking thought as he slipped into unconsciousness. They'll find your hand prints 'round my neck.... can't be too many people with hands that size...

When Charlie awoke, he found himself in a portakabin. The huge man was seated next to a small calor gas stove with a kettle boiling on it.

Charlie checked his neck. Not sore. He touched his head. Ouch!

The man turned towards him. "So, you're conscious, are you?"

Charlie sat up as best he could.

"Who are you? Why have you brought me here?" asked Charlie. "My mum'll have your guts for garters if she finds out you've kidnapped me. And my friend Hank will..."

"Hold it, hold it. Who's kidnapped you? What *are* you talking about?" The man now gave Charlie his full attention. "I think I should be the one asking the questions. For starters, what were you doing acting suspiciously in the graveyard?"

"Acting suspiciously?" Charlie was indignant. "I was looking for something I dropped earlier. I wasn't doing anything I shouldn't have been doing."

"Why'd you run then?" asked the man.

"You startled me," said Charlie. "That's all." He

wasn't about to admit he'd been scared out of his wits.

"What were you looking for?"

"None of your business," said Charlie, trying to be brave. The thing was, his head was throbbing so much, he could hardly stand the pain. He tried to get up.

"Sit down," said the man. "You've got a bit of a concussion. Your head's cut, though it doesn't need stitching. You'll be able to take the dressing off tomorrow but you'll have to make sure you keep it clean."

"Did you dress it for me?" Charlie asked.

"Course I did. Who do you think did it? I picked you up and carried you here. I dressed your wound. Now, are you going to tell me what were you looking for?"

"My sister's Bible," said Charlie, grudgingly. If the guy had taken care of him, as he said he had, he surely owed him a bit of courtesy.

"White one?" asked the man.

"Yes," Charlie brightened considerably. "Did you find it?"

The man dug into his trouser pocket and brought out Ace's Bible. "I found it earlier tonight when I was doing my rounds. I read the inscription inside and thought someone would be back for it. Though I didn't expect the person to return at the dead of night. Especially not when there'd been a murder committed here not more than a week ago."

Charlie stretched out his hand and took the Bible gratefully.

"Thanks, Mr… sorry, didn't quite catch your name."

"Felix Kittering," said the man. "And you are?"

"Charlie Christian. Sorry to have been so rude, Mr Kittering. Like I say, I was startled when you appeared and things just kinda went wrong from there."

Felix poured some boiling water into a mug and added a teabag. "Can I offer you some?" he asked Charlie.

Charlie shook his head.

"No thanks. So now will you tell me who you are?" he asked the older man.

Felix drank deeply from his mug and Charlie wondered idly why his lips didn't get burnt. Then just as quickly he wondered why he was having such a stupid thought.

"Night watchman. That's me," replied Felix. "Been employed by the church committee for the past six months. Been a spate of theft going on here, son. Petty thieving, you know the sort, but how folks can steal from a church is beyond me. So the committee got together and decided what they needed was a night watchman. Someone who was willing to stay out here all night every night and keep an eye on the comings and goings. Someone who wasn't afraid of ghosts." He laughed.

Charlie smiled. "I'm not afraid of ghosts, Mr Kittering, I didn't think for a minute you were a ghost. I don't really know what I thought. Anyway, why don't they just lock up the church and then they wouldn't need a watchman?"

"It's this new minister, Reverend Harvey. He believes the church should be open to the people twenty-four hours a day, seven days a week, just in case anyone needs to come and worship, spend some quiet time inside. So he won't hear of it. The doors have to be open at all times. "It's the people's church," is what he says. Why, many is the time lately I've found him wandering around the graveyard on his own at all hours. And when I ask him what he's looking for, he just smiles and says, 'the Lord's forgiveness'. He don't look like much of a sinner to me. Too hard on himself, he is."

Charlie nodded. "Do you know anything about the history of the church and cemetery, Mr Kittering?".

"Quite a lot," Felix replied. "What do you want to know?"

"Oh, nothing in particular," Charlie replied. He wasn't yet sure whether or not he trusted Mr Kittering and didn't want to arouse any suspicions regarding the Sinclair grave. He chose to lie. "I'm working on a school project during the holidays and it's about old buildings in Glasgow. I thought the church might make an interesting subject."

Felix nodded in agreement. "It certainly would. Anything you want to know, if I can help you out, I will. You come and see me anytime. I'm here every night from nine o'clock onwards."

Charlie stood up and held onto the edge of the chair for support.

"You okay?" asked Felix.

"I'll be fine," replied Charlie. "Just felt a bit dizzy when I stood up, that's all. I live fairly near here, so I'll be on my way now."

Felix accompanied him outside and said goodbye. "You sure you'll be all right?"

"I'll be fine," said Charlie, making sure the Bible was in his pocket. "See you again real soon, Mr Kittering," he said, as he began to make his way home.

Charlie looked at his reflection in the mirror. He hoped Mum wouldn't look in on him in the morning when she finished her night shift or she'd see the bandage and fly into a panic. He couldn't be bothered with the fuss. His head was fine but she'd insist he come in to the hospital to be checked. He'd try and stuff his head under the covers if he heard her come into the room.

His head still throbbed a bit but he knew the pain would ease. He took out his notes and looked for the part where he'd scribbled the quote that was inscribed on the Sinclair gravestone. There it was. Matthew: chapter 21, verse 12.

And Jesus went into the temple of God and cast out all them that sold and bought in the temple and overthrew the tables of the moneychangers.

Moneylenders! Albie Merrins had been a moneylender; a loan shark. But why should this verse be referred to on someone's gravestone? Gravestones usually carried words of comfort, words of loss, not threatening ones like these. Maybe 'G Sinclair' had also been involved in money lending. Who knows? Charlie's head throbbed and he lay down. He'd think about it while he rested and maybe make some more notes.

Five minutes later, he was fast asleep.

CHAPTER 7

ELIMINATION

CHARLIE called at Hank's office the following night and found him slumped in a chair staring despondently at the television.

"What's up?" asked Charlie as he joined him.

Hank pointed at the screen. Rachel had appeared again on the Dead Guy TV channel, which TG had managed to get on the air properly. Hank had even managed to video it this time. He'd been watching it over and over ever since, becoming more and more lonesome each time. Hank briefly explained Dead Guy TV to Charlie, who was used to taking all this spooky stuff in his stride now. He even guessed that TG was the brains behind it. He asked Hank who Rachel was.

"An old flame of mine. Someone I was very fond of back in LA. I cared for her very much." He looked at Charlie, his eyes full of sadness.

"Yeuch!" said Charlie unsympathetically. "You're in love! Look at you, mooning over a TV screen. One thing's for sure, you'll never catch me acting like that over a girl. Anyway…

if you can bear to tear yourself away from the screen… I found Ace's Bible last night. Though I had a little bit of an accident at the graveyard." He half smiled and indicated the cut on his head.

Hank didn't reply. Neither did he look up. The singer had been introduced on the show as 'Ellen Starling' but he was convinced she was Rachel. Rachel who was dead. She was the corpse that sang. He pressed the rewind button so he could watch again.

Charlie sighed. "Hank, are you listening to me?"

"Hmm…?" said Hank, without showing any interest.

"Hank," said Charlie, more insistently this time. "I've found out some more about the gravestone inscriptions. Listen to this…"

But Hank wasn't paying the slightest bit of attention to what Charlie was saying. He had pressed the play button on the video control and stared dreamily at the screen. Charlie picked up everything he'd emptied from his rucksack and started to leave. Hank was obviously going to be of no help whatsoever on this case. He'd have to go it alone.

"Why don't you pay a visit to Cowcaddens, if you're so keen to see this woman. Go up there and speak to her in person if you think it'll make you feel any better."

Hank pressed the pause button.

"Go where? Visit who?" he asked.

"It's a place, Hank. Cowcaddens is an area in Glasgow. It's where the TV studios are. If your ex-girlfriend is recording TV shows then that's where you'll find her," he said, as he closed the door behind him. Charlie was determined now to complete this case on his own.

Hank had heard every word Charlie had said. He was only playing dumb. Sure, he was besotted with the corpse that sang but that didn't mean he'd suddenly gone stupid. And yes, he was distracted by the reappearance of his Rachel. But he still held the Albie Merrins case in his head. He was still determined to help Albie's niece, Sally, who'd hired him. But he was also determined that everyone should think that Charlie had solved the case himself. That would go down very well with the Court Of Ghouls.

The next night was Friday and Charlie had

decided to pay a visit to the church youth club. He'd told his mum that morning.

"That's great," she smiled, putting down her newspaper. "You can take Annie with you."

"But Mum," protested Charlie. "Do I have to? It's not really her thing, is it?" He looked towards his younger sister. "Aren't you seeing some of your own friends tonight. Maybe you could invite some of them over. You could have them spend the night and I'll sleep on the sofa if you like."

Annie looked back at him. He *really* didn't want her to go to the youth club. He'd just offered to give up his bed for the night if she wouldn't go. That made up her mind. "I'd love to come to the youth club with you, Charlie." She smiled sweetly at him.

So, later that evening, brother and sister made their way towards the church.

"Why'd you bring your rucksack, Charlie?" asked Annie as she tried to keep up with him.

"It's got stuff in it that I need, Ace, okay? Now stop bugging me with stupid questions. And once we're inside I don't want you following me around, okay? I'll meet you at the exit when it's time to leave. Other than that I don't want to see you."

Jeez, thought Annie. Her older brother could be *so* charming. Just as well she was thick skinned!

They got inside the hall and were instantly separated. Annie recognised some kids from school and went to join them. They were supposed to be playing a game of netball but so far had spent their time chatting on the sidelines.

Charlie's plan was to mingle with his friends for a while then, when he knew Reverend Harvey to be otherwise occupied, he'd sneak off to his house and investigate. Good detective work was all down to elimination and he wanted to eliminate the good Reverend from his enquiries, before he moved on to the next suspect.

He played a game of table tennis with one of his friends but lost badly. His mind just wasn't on the game. He then joined the queue for the tuck shop. He bought some crisps and ate them noisily as he wandered around the hall.

He could see Reverend Harvey in a smaller hall just off the larger one he was standing in.

He was showing someone a yellow card, busily refereeing a five-a-side football match. A girl who was a little younger than Charlie bumped into him as she squeezed past. “Sorry,” she smiled, blushing as she spoke. “S’okay,” muttered Charlie, distractedly, as he pushed another handful of salt and vinegar crisps into his mouth.

He made his way to the exit, which he knew was only a short walk to the minister’s house. Reverend Jason Harvey watched him go.

CHAPTER 8

SUNSHINE IN GLASGOW

HANK looked at his watch. It was just after nine o'clock in the evening. He stood huddled in a doorway and watched as people arrived and left the TV studios.

He wondered if Dead Guy TV was broadcast from the main TV studios. It seemed highly unlikely that the ghost channel department would be situated right beside the normal stuff. But Charlie had suggested it was. And if Charlie had given him a clue, it was because TG wanted him to have that clue. Charlie would have had that thought put in his head by TG without his even being aware of it. Hank had a hunch that this was TG's way of helping him.

Hank dug his hands deeper into his pockets and shivered. He was freezing and he hadn't taken a lot of his flesh preserving 'potion' with him.

Just then TG himself tapped him on the shoulder.

"What you doing here Hank? Waiting on some dame?" he chuckled.

"Something like that. Tell me TG, what TV studio do you use for your channel – it wouldn't be here would it? Beside regular TV?"

"Where else? I'm a little short of cash these days, so I gotta piggy back on the human TV people's facilities."

"How do you explain that to them?"

"Easy, I don't," said TG, as if there could be no other answer.

"But don't they wonder who you are?"

"No. They are not even aware of my presence – or the presence of my technicians, or my crew, or my actors, or anybody."

"How come?"

TG laughed, looked at Hank and slapped him hard on the back.

"Eh, because we are all…dead! Wake up Mr Detective. You are not thinking tonight! We're all ghosts, remember? Invisible to all those still alive. Besides, our shows go out after, 'alive guys' all go home. So we come and go as we please."

Hank pondered that for a moment. It made sense. These things only stopped making sense when Hank forgot that he himself was dead.

"Gotta run," said TG, heading for the entrance of the studio. "Big show tonight. Special guests on the new chat show include JFK, Winston Churchill and Frank Sinatra! They've formed a great band, too. Man, you oughtta hear this Sinatra dude sing!" And with that TG disappeared.

Hank peered through the misty rain at a set of car headlights that were coming his way. A taxi drew up outside the studios and someone got out. Hank strained forward to try and see the passenger's face more clearly. He needn't have bothered. The minute the young woman started to walk he knew who it was. Rachel. He recognised her instantly.

He broke into a run, calling her name. Rachel stopped and turned to see what the commotion was. A man was running towards her, a man wearing a long 1950s style raincoat, a hat and a collar and tie that were way too big for him. He reached her and put out a hand to touch her. She smiled and took his hand. "Hank," she murmured as she buried her face in his coat, mixing her tears with the rain already on his collar.

They sat side by side in the studio café, sipping from large steaming mugs of coffee. Hank couldn't take his eyes from her face, couldn't believe that once more he was with her. Rachel put down her mug and touched Hank's face and whispered,

"I yearned for you so much, Hank. It was like I could see you and hear you but an invisible screen separated us. I even tried to sing you our song but no matter what I did I couldn't get you to notice that I was right beside you. It's been like a nightmare that's lasted fifty years."

Hank tried to remain unsentimental. But inside he felt like a prayer he'd long given up on had been answered. There had been so many times when he'd sensed her presence; so many times he'd heard her singing *Sleeping In The Sunlight.* But he'd put it down to his mind playing tricks on him. Could it have been that she'd really been there all the time?

"Rachel, I don't understand. How did you...?"

She traced the rim of her coffee cup with her finger and began to explain.

"It's a long story, Hank. After I was killed..."

Hank flinched.

"…I saw you falling to pieces. Long before you were shot dead, I watched your soul disintegrate. I saw you consumed by bitterness. I saw you become everything you hated in a cop. I saw you losing yourself. When you were killed I wanted to help, to remind you of who you really were before it was too late. So I approached the Court of Ghouls."

Hank glanced at her, a question in his eyes.

"Yep, I know those guys, too," she nodded. "Not the most attractive bunch I ever met but, hey, they did allow me to come back for a visit so I can't really complain."

A waitress approached to see if more coffee was needed but both of them shook their heads.

"Anyway," continued Rachel, getting back to her story, "they allowed me to come back, but only to say goodbye. And they set some conditions. I wasn't allowed to contact you. You had to find me. So the best plan I could come up with was to somehow appear on late night television and get you to hear our song; the one you'd done your best to forget. I knew TG of course. After all, he had collected my soul when I was killed back in 1950. I thought he might be able to provide clues to your whereabouts."

"How'd you figure that?"

"I was a detective, remember? Anyway, he told me about his TV channel, and about a talent show he was putting together. He made some calls and got me an audition. I was up against this truck driver from Memphis, a real good-looking guy, with an amazing voice. He was called, 'Elvis' something or other. He seemed to think he was destined to win. But the judges picked me. That meant I would get my big chance to sing live on Dead Guy TV. You knew singing was my hobby, right? But I didn't think I'd beat that Elvis character. He seemed pretty stunned that he'd lost. He accused TG of fixing it."

"TG's good at fixing things that ain't broke, if you get my drift."

"Yeah, I got that impression! Still I wasn't going to ask for a re-run."

"But why, Rachel? Why couldn't we connect? It sounds like we've been close to each other even in death."

"Don't you see Hank? The good man who never broke the law – that Hank Kane simply vanished when I died. The fearsome, vengeful cop you became was someone I didn't recognise, couldn't connect with. I tried to reach you with our song – but you couldn't hear me because you'd become someone else. You see, Hank, we'll never be together until you become your decent self again. That's what I've been trying to tell you for over fifty years."

Hank stared at her face. It still looked like her flesh was melting, just like when he'd first seen her on Dead Guy TV. He wanted to play it cool, for her sake. He knew he was too useful to TG for TG to ever let him cross over to Detective Heaven. He knew that that would break her heart. *How* did he know? Because it was breaking his.

"When do you have to go back?" asked Hank coldly.

"Now," she replied, her cold manner matching his. She'd been his equal in every way.

"You're staring at my face Hank. I know what you see. You see the flesh falling as my face becomes that of a skeleton, don't you?"

Hank was now looking away, annoyed that he'd made himself so obvious.

"But Hank, look in this mirror." Rachel pulled a small mirror from her bag and moved 'round to sit beside Hank. She held the mirror so that Hank could see her face in it. Her face was beautiful! Her reflection in the mirror looked exactly as she had done fifty years ago!

Hank was stunned. He felt it all coming back to him; the pain he felt as he held her dead body in his arms, her singing, him trying to teach her the piano, their wonderful life together, everything. The Dead Detective felt his own face melt a little as a tear fell down his left cheek. Rachel put the mirror away.

"In the mirror," said Hank, "that was the real you, Rachel, not this singing corpse."

"And the only Hank Kane who'll will ever see the real me again, is the *real* Hank Kane, the man I knew and loved. This decaying corpse that I've become, that's the only Rachel you'll remember, unless you can solve your cases the 'Hank Kane Way'. I'll be waiting Hank. But I can't wait forever. Do the right thing."

Just then TG walked up to their table.

"Ok, lovebirds, party's over. C'mon sugar, it's time for your part of the bargain. The band's all warmed up. It's time for your number – and remember, this is 'live'!"

Rachel stood up and looked at Hank, who stayed seated. She wanted to say more but she knew there was no point. Hank wasn't listening. This cold, bitter Hank Kane was a stranger to her, a shell of the person she'd once loved.

Hank didn't look up until she'd walked away. He watched as TG took her arm and gave her some last minute coaching for her singing performance. He'd known he was hurting her and yet he couldn't stop himself.

TG looked back at Hank and Hank saw that TG had a look of pity on his face. Was it really all for the best? Was there really no chance of Hank escaping TG's twilight world and meeting Rachel in Detective Heaven one day? This cold Hank Kane decided it was time to warm to the task. The band had started Rachel's tune, *Sleeping In The Sunlight*. He walked out of the studio into the rain-sodden night with the song crashing around his head,

"...Now I know,
What death is like,
It's just like sleeping,
Sleeping in the sunlight..."

"Sunlight? In Glasgow? Are you kidding?" thought the Dead Detective. Boy, did he miss LA.

CHAPTER 9

THE MORE YOU KILL...

AS Charlie had hoped, the door to the minister's house was open and he was able to walk inside. He moved quickly, unsure of what he was looking for but hoping to find something that would help his investigation. He could almost hear Hank's voice saying, "clues don't find *you* – you gotta find *them*!"

He jumped when he heard a noise in the kitchen but found it was only the minister's cat returning home via the cat-flap. He briefly imagined Reverend Harvey's cat out preaching to all the other cats in the street, scolding the tomcats as they fought each other in the moonlight. He chuckled irreverently.

The minister wasn't the tidiest of people; magazines were scattered on the floor, coffee cups littered every available work surface in the kitchen, and his bed was unmade. Charlie heard another noise and ignored it. Probably just the cat again. He was startled when a voice behind him asked:

"Anything I can help you with, Charlie?"

He turned to see Reverend Harvey standing in the doorway.

Seated in the tiny living room, Charlie was very uncomfortable. Reverend Harvey had told him to sit down and, although he had been perfectly polite, Charlie knew he was very angry at finding someone in his house. The minister sat across from him and Charlie could see his hands were shaking.

"Reverend Harvey, Jason, I'm sorry, really I am. I didn't mean to trespass, honestly I didn't, but I did look for you in the church hall to ask if I could have a look 'round your house and I couldn't find you. So I hoped you wouldn't mind if I just..." he tailed off lamely.

The minister held up his hand to indicate silence and Charlie could see his hand was shaking with controlled anger. Charlie was in deep trouble and he knew it. He'd better shut up and concentrate on finding a way out.

"Albie Merrins," began Reverend Harvey. "That's the reason you're here, isn't it. Nothing to do with school projects."

Charlie nodded his head. No point in lying, he decided.

"You want to know the story of Albie, do you? Well, I'll tell you. The Merrins family were a very bad lot but I'm sure you've discovered that already, young Sherlock. But did you know that Albie and his brother, Lex, were actually orphans? They were brought up by Mrs Merrins or 'Ma Merrins' as she was better known. The Merrins had figured they might need sons to run their gangster business one day. Albie's brother, Lex, had gone straight, and opened a wee general store. He'd disowned the Merrins and taken back his real name, which was Sinclair."

"Sinclair?" asked Charlie, "Albie's body was left next to the grave of Geoffrey Sinclair!"

"That's right, Charlie. Lex had married and he and his wife were happy, eventually expanding the shop and taking on more workers. Then times got hard and the family borrowed more money than they could ever hope to pay back. They were at their wits end and with Lex's wife pregnant, they needed a way out.

"And that way out was, Albie Merrins, Lex's caring brother. He offered to loan a large sum of money to the family, which they accepted gratefully. Little did they know what they'd let themselves in for. The interest rates on the loan were so high that the family struggled to find the weekly repayments. One by one they were forced to sack their workers. Profits were down and their debt grew higher and higher. The stress drove Lex to an early grave. His poor wife was so upset that she went into labour prematurely and died giving birth to twins, a boy and a girl. The baby girl died a few hours later. The nurses called her 'Angel Heart', as she'd been born with a birth mark on her cheek in the shape of a heart...". His voice shook slightly and he paused.

Charlie shifted in his seat. Everything Harvey had told him had been said with very little emotion. It was only when he looked directly at him that Charlie could see his eyes were filled with the deepest sorrow. Charlie looked away, and the minister began to speak again.

"And so, following in the family tradition, the boy was placed in an orphanage until a suitable family came along and rescued him. He took on the name of his new family, grew up with them, and ... eventually... entered the Church."

"You?" asked Charlie, shocked.

The minister nodded his head.

"That's right. My father was Geoffrey Sinclair and he and my mother were killed by Albie Merrins. My real name's Martin Sinclair and I was the one who wrote the farewell letter to the paper."

"So the quotes on the gravestone - " began Charlie.

" - were chosen by me," finished Reverend Harvey. "'Vengeance is mine', has long been one of my favourites," he smiled, "only God was taking just a little too long to do the repaying in my opinion."

"So you killed Merrins?" asked Charlie.

"Right here in this very room. I killed my own uncle," the minister nodded. "Killing is in my blood, it seems. Only things went a bit wrong. His body wasn't supposed to be found in the graveyard but Kittering, the night watchman, was doing his rounds when I tried to move the body so I had to dump it in a hurry. Didn't matter, though. The police thought someone had deliberately placed the body there because Forensics told them it had been moved. They didn't know that it had only been moved from *inside* the church."

"Why did you wait this long to kill him, if you'd always wanted to kill him?" asked Charlie.

"I never wanted to kill anyone Charlie. All my life, I've struggled to forgive him. That's why I became a Christian, to forgive and to lose these feelings of hate and rage. But then Albie came around and reminded me of my father's unpaid debt. Imagine, Charlie! He was behaving as if *I* owed *him*! He put a knife to my throat! He only put it down when I told him where the collection box was! He thought it was funny that there was only twenty-six pounds in it. As he was putting the money in his pocket, I picked up the knife. I don't remember anything else, except him lying on the floor, bleeding to death. Something, or someone inside me killed Albie Merrins. And I'm not sorry. I yearn to be, though. A real Christian would be. Instead of being sorry, I read about other gangs and other gangsters and I want to kill them."

"How? By becoming a bigger bad guy than the

bad guys? What would that prove, except that evil wins twice over?" said Charlie.

"All I can tell you is I'm glad I've been caught. God only knows what I would have gone on to do. And of all the people to be caught by, I'm glad it's a 'Christian'."

There was a knock at the door.

"Who is it?" Harvey called out.

"Hank Kane, Reverend."

"And Annie Christian!" shouted Annie.

"Looks like you're outnumbered by Christians, two to one," said Charlie.

"At least two to one, Charlie, at least."

The minister opened the front door of the house and Hank and Annie came in. Hank looked at Reverend Harvey.

"We don't need cuffs, Reverend, do we?" asked Hank.

"No Mr Kane."

"Well, do you mind if we all wait together for the police?" said Hank.

They sat in silence, trying to come to terms with the situation.

"Mr Kane," asked the minister, "why did you get involved in this case?"

"Well, I don't pick the cases, Reverend, they pick me. It's a long story, don't ask."

"Mr Kane, I know more about you than you think."

"Oh yeah?"

"Oh yeah, indeed. You see, Mr Kane, being a minister means dealing with a lot of death. And in the course of dealing with death, I've sensed the presence of spirits, ghosts if you like. They seem to be conjured up by their loved ones left behind, particularly in times of great stress."

"So what's this got to do with knowing me?"

"I'm a little bit psychic, so I know you are a ghost."

With that there was silence in the room once more. Charlie and Annie wondered what Hank would do next! His cover was blown. They were amazed how calmly he seemed to accept this.

"I know more about you than you think, Reverend," said Hank. "You're a lost soul. Oh, don't get me wrong. You ain't no ghost. You are very much alive. But the *real* you, or the best part of you, died with your sister and your mother when she gave birth to you. And you've felt alone ever since – "

" – Not *felt* alone, *been* alone, Mr Kane."

"No. *Felt* alone. You were so consumed by bitterness, that you couldn't sense the family that tried to save you."

"Save me? From what?"

"From yourself."

"And what 'family' are you talking about, Mr Kane? My family is dead, remember?"

"You asked me why I took this case. Well, not long after you killed Albie, a beautiful woman visited my office, saying she wanted the killer caught before he killed again. There's an old saying, 'the more you kill, the more you die'. Maybe that lady was trying to save what was left of you before you killed again."

"Who was she?" asked the minister, shaking, though he already knew the answer.

"My guess is that she was your twin sister."

"My sister's dead, Mr Kane," said Harvey with tears falling down his cheeks.

"She's just sleeping in the sunlight, Reverend, just sleeping in the sunlight. She looked just like you, except – "

" No! Don't say it!" pleaded the minister.

"Except for the birth mark, the one in the shape – "

" – Of a heart," finished Harvey, recovering his composure.

Charlie and Annie were transfixed. Once again, Hank had seemed to know the whole story all along.

"Way I see it, Reverend?" said Hank, "is this is the best thing that could have happened to you. Maybe now you'll realise that you're not alone. We all got someone looking out for us on the other side. We just got to let them get through. Just got to be ourselves, our true selves." Hank was talking to himself as much as to Reverend Harvey.

The police sirens sounded just as Hank finished speaking. They came in and were leading Reverend Harvey away when he stopped to say something to Hank.

"When you see my sister, Mr Kane, will you tell her 'thanks' from me?"

Hank smiled at him and said, "Tell her yourself, Martin."

CHAPTER 10

THE REAL HANK KANE

HANK was back in the Court of Ghouls and he was impatient. Charlie had solved the case and was full of his own self importance for having done so. At least that was the story TG had instructed everyone to stick to. The door opened and Hank and TG were summoned. Jeez, these guys get uglier every time I see them, Hank thought as he took a seat.

"Please stand, Detective Kane," hissed the vampire, his white skin glowing against the redness of his eyes.

Hank stood reluctantly. Who did these guys think they were?

"Your judge and jury," answered the twins in unison. "That's who we are, Mr Kane."

Darn it, thought Hank, he'd forgotten they could read his mind.

He looked at the fourth judge. "Were you mauled by a lion?" he asked. "I mean, I hope you don't mind me asking, but the skin's literally been torn from your face. You look really awful..."

"Not a lion, a werewolf," answered the judge dryly. Now let's get down to business."

"The Bible," he said, looking directly at Hank.

"Yes?" Hank asked. "What about it?"

"Did young Christian drop it at the crime scene or did you place it there?"

"Look, the boy's young, he's just learning. He missed the inscription first time around and I knew he needed a second look…"

The vampire interrupted. "Answer the question, Detective Kane. Did you or did you not place the bible at the scene?"

Hank glanced at TG, who refused to meet his gaze.

"But you don't understand. The kid's new to this game, he's not sure what to look for. I only…"

The judges conferred. And after what seemed like an eternity, the vampire judge surprised everyone by saying,

"Kane, your cheating this time can hardly be called serious. And Mr Christian would test the patience of a saint! We've decided therefore that we are going to give you a break and let you cross over. Congratulations!"

No-one celebrated, as they all knew how sick a sense of humour the judges had.

Hank looked at TG. He knew that TG had kept his side of the bargain, for once!

"Why TG? Why this time?"

"I saw the way you looked at that dame. She really is your soul mate, Hank. Good luck!"

But then Hank surprised everyone. Just as the judges were walking out of the court, Hank shouted for everyone's attention.

"Listen up, guys. Everyone? I have something to say."

They all filed back in, none too happy.

"Well Kane," asked the vampire judge, "what do you want to say?"

"I can't go."

There were gasps from every corner of the court!

"What do you mean?" shouted TG.

"I *did* cheat. I learned the name of the killer while at *The Cesspit.* I asked someone who knew, and they told me. They didn't think I'd heard. I made a big fuss about something else at the time but I'd heard fine. I'll tell you what I learned on this case. I learned that I have to solve crime the 'Hank Kane Way'. I have to be myself. Only then will the real me meet up with Rachel. Only then will I truly be in Detective Heaven. Only then…"

Hank's inspiring speech was interrupted by TG's solitary hand clapping. Hank had got so carried away, that he didn't notice that the court had emptied while he was confessing! He was insulted that no-one had wanted to hear what he had to say.

TG climbed into the dock, where Hank was standing. Hank was still mumbling about how rude it had been of the Court to leave in the middle of his speech. TG had his arm around Hank's shoulder, guiding him out of the courtroom, murmuring, "I know, I know. They are a very irreverent bunch. Wouldn't know decency if it bit them on the butt…"

The pair of them went out the door of the building and walked down the steps. Hank was busy telling TG how he was going to be different from now on. TG was doing his best to try and show some interest.

"I know, I know…" he said as he and Hank disappeared into the Glasgow night. For a few moments, Hank's voice could still be heard telling TG that he was a changed man; until it was drowned out by the sound of rain pounding the pavements they walked on.

The End

OTHER TITLES IN THE DEAD DETECTIVE SERIES:

DEAD AND UNBURIED

Los Angeles 1953... and Private Detective Hank Kane doesn't know what's hit him. Lying face down on the same street he was just running down, he realises he's been shot. But instead of the morgue, Hank finds himself in the Court of Ghouls, in front of a Vampire judge and a jury of ghosts! He's on trial for cheating on his last case. His punishment? To get back to 'life' and solve a case honestly. Lippy 12-year-old Charlie Christian is assigned as his apprentice detective! The question is not, "will they solve the case?" but "will they solve it honestly?"

SIX FEET UNDER

Hank falls and knocks himself out while chasing a thief from his office. He's forgotten to take his "medicine bottle" with him and his flesh starts disappearing, revealing his bony white skeleton underneath. Everybody is talking about the "well-dressed Skeleton" found lying in the street. His old-fashioned 1940s clothes and hat look very strange. The police, after forensic tests, have the body buried. Is this really the end of Hank Cane? It will be, unless Charlie can work out Hank's secret code in the letter in his desk drawer, marked "ONLY TO BE OPENED IN AN EMERGENCY". If this isn't an emergency what is? But can Charlie handle all the secrets in the letter?

DEAD LOSS

Hank gets a visit from the ghost of murder victim Tony Falco, begging for help. Tony, a cat burglar, had stolen jewels on him when he died and the Court of Ghouls won't let Tony into Bandit Heaven until he returns them. Just one problem though – no-one found Falco's body. It's lost! Hank thinks that the Grim Reaper might have some clues. His apprentice, Charlie, is desperate to solve the case without help of any "dead guys", but he disappears! Now the Grim Reaper and Falco have a body full of loot to find – and the apprentice too!

THROW AWAY THE KEY

"Help me... please, help me!" A voice identifying itself only as "The Prisoner" keeps calling Hank's phone, pleading for help. Despite being asked why, the panicking voice just keeps calling. Charlie introduces Hank to the latest technology in phone tapping and they listen carefully to the background noises, searching for clues. They get worried when they begin to recognise some sounds, which are too familar for comfort. The Prisoner is very, very close to home!!

GHOST CAR 49

The siren from an old-fashioned American police car is heard echoing around the streets at night. The sound of screeching tyres, blaring police radio, 1940s jazz music and constant gunfire freak out the local residents. Needless to say, Charlie gets the call: "Better get over here, Kid. Looks like we've got something." But how will they bring Car 49 to a halt? And who is at the wheel?!

THE DEAD DETECTIVE SERIES

Dead and Unburied	1-904684-00-9
Six Feet Under	1-904684-01-7
Dead Loss	1-904684-02-5
The Corpse That Sang	1-904684-03-3
Throw Away The Key	1-904684-04-1
Ghost Car 49	1-904684-05-X

www.booksnoir.com

www.deaddetective.com

Hey guys! Hank Kane here. Check out my website www.deaddetective.com *to keep up to date with my interactive e-book* Web of Intrigue, *an internet adventure where you, the reader, can help me on the case.*

P.S. You'd better be good!